A Cassava Republic Press edition 2017

First published in Belgium and Holland by Clavis Uitgeverij,
Hasselt – Amsterdam, 2010, Copyright © 2010, Clavis Uitgeverij

English translation from the Dutch by Clavis Publishing Inc. New York
Copyright © 2011 for the English language edition:
Clavis Publishing Inc. New York

Every Girl is a Princess written and illustrated by Mylo Freeman
Original title: Ieder meisje een prinses
Translated from the Dutch by Clavis Publishing

ISBN 978-1-911115-38-0

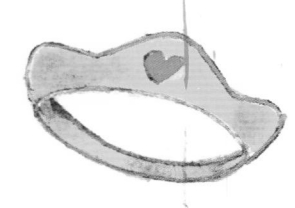

A CIP catalogue record for this book is available from the British Library.

www.cassavarepublic.biz

Every Girl is A Princess

MYLO FREEMAN

CASSAVA REPUBLIC

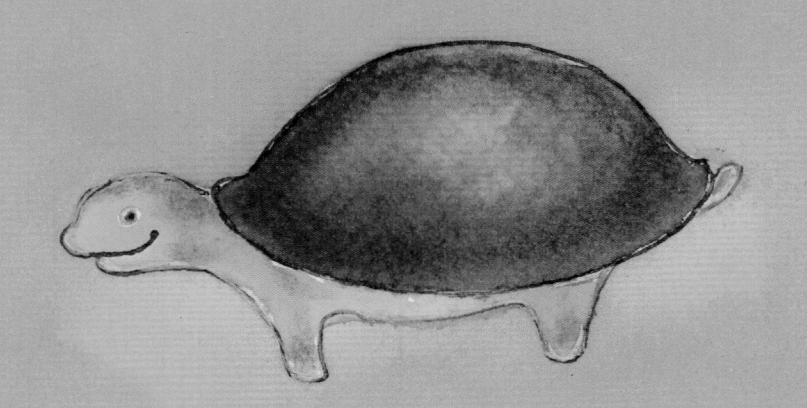

This is Princess Naomi.
She loves turtles.
On her crown is a rainbow.
Could this be her crown?

This is Princess Isabel.
She likes pigs the most.
She has a little heart on her crown.
Might this be her little crown?

The next one is Princess Adinda.
She adores snakes.
On her crown is a star.
Could this be her crown?

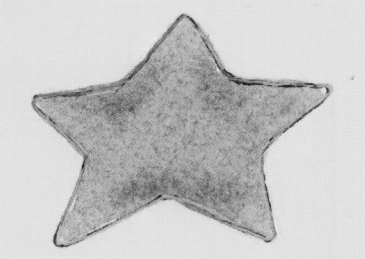

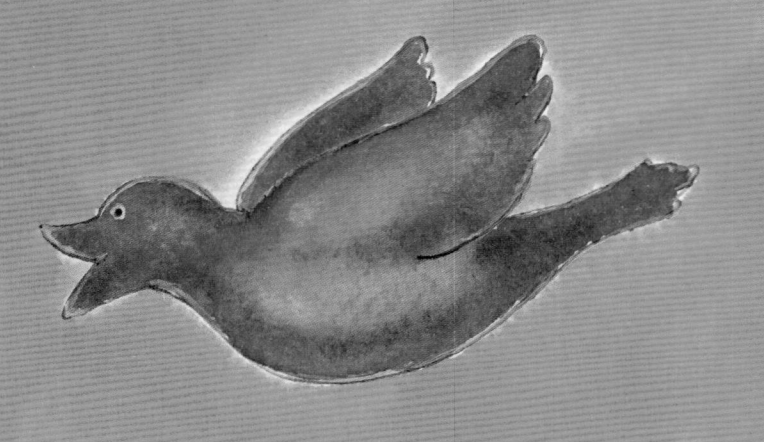

Look, it's Princess Rosalina.
She is fond of birds.
She's got a flower on her crown.
So this is her crown, isn't it?

And this is Princess Ushi.
She loves the way fish swim.
On her crown are pearls.
Could this be her crown?

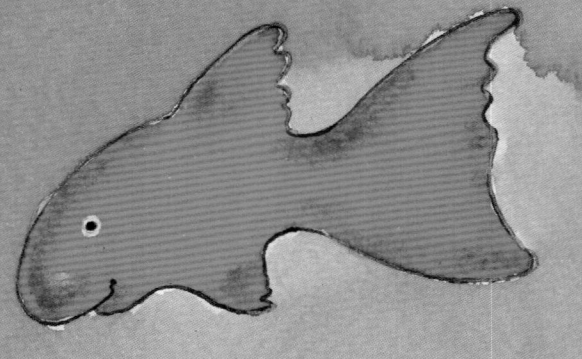

Each princess is wearing her own crown ...

But who does this crown belong to?

Guess what, this crown is for you!
Because every girl is a princess, isn't she?
(And every boy is a prince.)

Look and see for yourself if you don't believe it!